THE PUPPY PLACE

ZIG & ZAG

Don't miss any of these other stories by Ellen Miles!

Angel

Bandit

Barney

Baxter

Bear

Bella

Bentley

Biggie

Bitsy

Bonita

Boomer

Bubbles and Boo

Buddy

Champ

Chewy and Chica

Cocoa

Cody

Cooper

Cuddles

Daisy

Donut

Edward

Flash

Fluffy & Freckles

Gizmo

Goldie

Gus

Honey

Jack

Jake

Kodiak

Liberty

Lily

Lola

Louie

Lucky

Lucy

Maggie and Max

Miki

Mocha

Molly

Moose

Muttley

Nala

Noodle

Oscar

Patches

Princess

Pugsley

Rascal

Rocky

Roxy

Rusty

Scout

Shadow

Snowball

Sparky

Spirit

Stella

Sugar, Gummi, and Lollipop

Sweetie

Teddy

Ziggy

Zipper

THE PUPPY PLACE

ZIG & ZAG

ELLEN
MILES

SCHOLASTIC INC.

Copyright © 2022 by Ellen Miles
Cover art by Tim O'Brien
Original cover design by Steve Scott

All rights reserved. Published by Scholastic Inc., *Publishers since 1920*. SCHOLASTIC and associated logos are trademarks and/or registered trademarks of Scholastic Inc.

ISBN 978-1-338-78186-1

10 9 8 7 6 5 4 3 2 1   22 23 24 25 26

Printed in the U.S.A.   40
First printing 2022

CHAPTER ONE

Fwoosh! With a great heave, Lizzie Peterson swept a big pile of leaves onto the tarp spread out on the lawn. Then she leaned on her rake and let out a sigh. She had filled this tarp five times already, dragging each load of leaves to the back corner of the yard where Dad used them to make compost. How many more loads would she have to rake and drag before she was finished?

Raking was definitely not one of Lizzie's favorite activities. It wasn't how it looked in the adorable photos of kids jumping into huge crunchy piles or tossing colorful leaves into the air. It was hard work. Her shoulders hurt. She had blisters on her hands even though she was wearing the gloves Mom had made her put on. Her brothers were being super annoying and not at all helpful. And on top of it all, her hair was full of leaves—not the colorful red and orange ones like in the adorable pictures, just plain old brown, crackly, musty leaves. The kind there were tons of in this yard, just waiting to be raked.

Why did trees have to drop their leaves, anyway? Why couldn't she live in the middle of an evergreen forest, or out in the middle of a prairie, or on an island with palm trees? If Mom and Dad knew what she was thinking, they'd remind her how lucky she was to live in a nice big house with a nice big yard full of nice big trees. Lizzie knew that. She knew she was lucky. She just wished someone else would do the raking.

The Bean, her youngest brother, was too young. He had a little-kid toy rake, but he wasn't much actual help. In reality, he just messed up Lizzie's neat piles and made the job take even longer. And he spent most of the time shouting and laughing and running and wrestling with Charles, her middle brother. Charles wasn't much help, either, even though Lizzie knew that he was old enough. Mostly he just fooled around with the Bean.

At least Lizzie did have one pal out there in the yard: her puppy, Buddy. She looked around now, wondering where he'd gotten to. "Buddy!" she called. A pair of perky ears popped out of a leaf pile. Buddy shook himself off and ran to Lizzie, his tongue lolling as he grinned a doggy grin. His brown coat shone in the sun. He sniffed at her hands, looking up at her expectantly.

"You want a treat, don't you?" Lizzie rummaged in her pocket, found half a small biscuit, and tossed it to him. Buddy caught it in midair, crunched it up, gulped it down, and then sniffed at her hand again as if asking for seconds.

Lizzie laughed and scratched him between the ears. Buddy always cheered her up. All dogs did, but especially this dog, her own dog, the very best dog in the history of the universe.

That cheering-up ability was one of the reasons Lizzie was dog-crazy. Who could ever be sad or cranky or worried for long with a puppy nearby? That was why she had convinced her parents that the Petersons should be a foster family. Now they were known all over Littleton for taking care of puppies who needed help. Lost puppies, abandoned puppies, injured puppies, puppies who were too wild, puppies whose people had to move away: they all showed up at the Petersons'.

Lizzie and her brothers and her parents took care of these puppies and did their best to find the perfect home for each one. Buddy had started out as one of their foster puppies—along with his mom and two sisters. It had not taken long for Lizzie and her family to figure out that Buddy's perfect home was right here with them. He was part of the family now, and he'd seen many other puppies come and go.

The "go" part? There was no question that it was always hard to say good-bye to the puppies they'd cared for. It was the hardest part of the whole thing! But having Buddy made it a little easier to see the other puppies leave. And, of course, it helped to know that they were going to fantastic homes where they would be truly loved and wanted, just like Buddy was.

"Isn't that right, Buddy?" Lizzie asked now, ruffling his ears. She scritched the heart-shaped white spot on his chest, remembering how she'd fallen in love with him the second she first saw it.

Buddy squirmed away and ran back to his leaf

pile, ready to take another dive. Lizzie had thrown his favorite squeaky football in there, and he still hadn't found it. "Find it, Buddy!" she called. "Find that toy!" Buddy loved playing hide-and-seek with his toys. Lizzie played with him indoors, too, tucking his favorite stuffed duck under the couch or behind a chair. He'd race around the room, sniffing and pawing at everything while his tail wagged double time. He always looked so proud when he finally found the toy. He'd bring it to Lizzie, his head and tail held high. Thinking about it, Lizzie felt her heart swell. She loved her puppy so much.

"Buddy! Buddy!" Charles and the Bean galloped across the backyard to help Buddy find his toy. Just as they got to the leaf pile, Buddy burrowed his nose down into the leaves, pulled out the football, and took off with it, looking over his shoulder to make sure the boys were chasing him.

Charles and the Bean shouted and waved their arms and tumbled into Lizzie's neat leaf piles as they tried to tackle the puppy.

Lizzie harrumphed and crossed her arms, shaking her head as she watched them. She loved her brothers, she really did. But why did they have to act like such—such *boys* sometimes? Would a sister be running around the yard screaming her head off as she chased the dog? Would a sister think that fart jokes were the funniest thing ever? Would a sister always grab the biggest slice of cake or the best piece of bacon? Well, maybe. Why not? Girls could be just as wild and gross and greedy as boys could. Lizzie had friends who had sisters, and they complained about them all the time. Still, she'd always wished she had at least one, if not three, like the March sisters in *Little Women*.

"Hi, kids!" Lizzie looked up to see Mom

standing on the deck. "Come sit with me. We need to talk." *Uh-oh.* Lizzie thought Mom looked serious. Lizzie checked behind her to see how the yard looked where she'd raked it. Mom was kind of picky about doing it the right way. But it looked fine—actually, it looked great. That part of the lawn was tidy and neat, ready for winter.

Lizzie looked back at Mom.

Mom was still frowning. "We need to talk," she repeated. "All of us." She raised her hands to her mouth, megaphone-style. "Boys!" she called.

They didn't hear her—or at least they didn't pay attention.

Mom put two fingers into her mouth and let out a shrieking whistle.

The boys stopped in their tracks, looked up, and ran right over, with Buddy bounding along.

Lizzie had to laugh. She loved that her mother

could whistle like that, and it always worked: with boys, with dogs, with anything. Lizzie had tried to learn many times, but so far all she ever got was a disappointing *thwww* sound.

"We need to talk," Mom said again, when they were all gathered on the deck steps.

"About what?" Lizzie asked.

"About a foster—" Mom said.

Lizzie and Charles exchanged a glance, grinning at each other. The Bean clapped his hands and jumped up and down. This was one of the most exciting parts of fostering: finding out all about their newest puppy. "What breed is it?" "How old?" "Girl or boy?" they shouted, all at the same time. Mom held up her hands.

"Hold on," Mom said. "I didn't say we were getting a puppy. I said we need to discuss it. Here's the thing: it's not just a foster puppy. It's more like, well, a fostering situation. One that we really have to consider carefully."

"Huh?" Lizzie had no idea what her mom might be talking about. "What do you mean, 'situation'?"

Her mom sighed. "It's two puppies. Sisters."

CHAPTER TWO

Now Lizzie couldn't help jumping up and down with excitement, just like the Bean. "Two! Yay! Two puppies equals double fun!"

Mom held up her hand. "See, this is exactly what we need to talk about because that's not always true, and we know it. Don't we?" She raised her eyebrows. "Remember Chewy and Chica?" she asked, touching her first finger. "Double trouble, not double fun. And what about Sugar, Gummi, and Lollipop? That was so ridiculous, trying to take care of three dogs at once."

Lizzie shook her head. "That's not how I

remember it," she said. "I thought we had a blast with all those puppies. And we found them fantastic homes, too." She bit her lip. Maybe it had been a little hectic at times, and maybe she had sometimes felt like she'd taken on too much—but it really had been fun, and it had all worked out in the end.

"O-kay," Mom said. "The thing is, I have an important deadline coming up on an article I've been working on for weeks." Mom was a reporter for the local paper, *The Littleton News.* "I just don't think it's the time to take on two puppies."

Lizzie appreciated that Mom had told them about the puppies, even though she thought the timing wasn't right. After all, she could have just said no, and never even told Lizzie and Charles. "We'll do everything!" Lizzie promised. "Walk them, feed them, play with them, train them—"

Charles was nodding. "You'll barely even know they're here!" he said.

Mom smiled. "Except maybe when you two are at school and the Bean is at preschool and Dad's at work and I'm all on my own here—oh, except for Buddy and a couple of puppies?" She ruffled Charles's hair.

"Just tell us more about them," Lizzie pleaded. "Some puppies are easier than others. Maybe these will be nice, calm puppies who don't need much attention."

"Hmm, let's see if I can remember," said Mom. She didn't really know her dog breeds—at least, not the way Lizzie did. "They're some type of spaniel," Mom said, closing her eyes as she tried to think.

Lizzie nodded, trying to keep a smile on her face in case Mom opened her eyes. Most spaniels were pretty active dogs. "Do you remember what kind?" she asked.

Mom frowned, thinking, and then opened her eyes. "Um, Brittany, maybe? Brittany spaniel? Is that a thing? Know anything about them?"

Lizzie gulped, still trying to keep that smile pasted to her face. Brittanies were some of the most hyper of all the spaniels. They were bred for bird hunting and had the energy to run all day through forests and marshes. "Well," she said, "they're—um—they're really smart," she said. She wasn't lying. Brittanies were known for their intelligence—and for their talent for getting into all sorts of trouble, too. "And cute! Really cute! They're not too big, either. Kind of medium-sized, with floppy ears and pretty white-and-brown spotted coats. Or black spots. Sometimes their spots are black." She was babbling now, as her thoughts raced. Was she remembering something about

Brittany spaniels being heavy shedders, also? The kind of dogs that leave hairs all over everything? Mom definitely didn't need to hear that. "Oh, and they're known for being really sweet and loyal," she finished, finally. She wasn't really sure about that part—but didn't it apply to most dogs?

Lizzie's mouth was beginning to ache with all the smiling.

Thankfully, Charles spoke up just then. "Can't we at least meet them?" he asked. "Wouldn't that help us to decide?"

"Yes!" Lizzie said. Mentally, she took back every bad thing she had thought about her brother. "Great point, Charles. It's only fair to give these puppies a chance, right?"

Mom looked doubtful. "Well," she said. "You know what will happen if we meet them. It'll be hard to say no."

"If they don't seem right for our family, we don't

have to take them," said Lizzie. "Please? Can we at least meet them?"

"Pleeeeeease?" echoed Charles, leaning against Mom.

"Pease pease pease pease pease," said the Bean, holding Mom's hand and looking up at her with his most irresistible expression.

"Fine." Mom stood up and brushed herself off. "We'll meet them. But no matter what, we're not going to take them home with us today, got it? We'll come home and discuss it, as a family."

Lizzie spun around in a circle. She was too excited to stand still. "Right, right, right," she said. "When can we go? Can we go now?"

Mom sighed. "Sure," she said.

"I get frontsies," Charles yelled.

Lizzie rolled her eyes. Sure, she and her brother often argued over who got to sit in the front row of the back of the van, next to the Bean in his car seat. But on a day like this—honestly, who cared? "It's all yours," she said as she put her rake away. "Buddy," she called. "Want to go for a ride?"

"Oh, noo—" Mom began. But Buddy had already dashed over, wearing his biggest grin and wagging his tail hard. Buddy loved to go for rides. "Maybe not this time," said Mom. "With all three of you, and—"

"Two puppies, on the way home! Yes!" Lizzie said, throwing up both hands so her brothers could give her high fives. "Okay, Buddy, Mom's right. You wait here." She led him inside and gave him three biscuits to make up for it. She knew he would be disappointed—for about a second. Then he would probably curl up for a nap.

"So, where are we going, anyway?" Lizzie asked as she buckled into her seat. "I would have heard if there were puppies at Caring Paws, so that can't be it." Caring Paws was the animal shelter where Lizzie volunteered.

Mom shook her head. "It's Julie's sister," she said. "You remember Julie, my friend from work? The sports editor? I guess her sister, Tracy, is always trying different schemes to make money. Last summer she was selling tie-dyed socks on Etsy. Before that she had a business caring for people's fish—she's always been good with fish, according to Julie. But I guess there weren't enough people who needed fish-sitters."

Lizzie giggled. But what her mother said next made the smile disappear from Lizzie's face.

"Well, anyway, I guess her latest scheme is . . ." Mom paused, and her eyes met Lizzie's in the rearview mirror. "Breeding puppies," she finished.

CHAPTER THREE

"Noooo!" Lizzie moaned.

"I knew you'd be upset," said her mom.

"Of course I am," said Lizzie. "You can't just start breeding puppies out of nowhere. You have to learn about it so you know what you're doing."

"Not to mention—" said Mom, as if she knew exactly what Lizzie was going to say next.

"Not to mention," said Lizzie, "there are already so many puppies and dogs who need homes. Breeding dogs just to make money just isn't—isn't—" She tried to remember how Ms. Dobbins, the director of Caring Paws, would put it. "Responsible," she finally burst out.

Mom nodded. "I know, I know," she said. "And I think Tracy knows, too. She's overwhelmed. She finally found homes for three puppies, but there are two left, sisters." She sighed. "I probably shouldn't have brought you with me. This was a bad idea, bringing all of you along to this woman's house."

Lizzie sat up straight in her seat. No matter what, she really, really wanted to foster these puppies. The first step was meeting them. She didn't want Mom to turn around now and head home. "I promise I won't say a peep," she said, pretending to zip her lip. "And—and Charles and the Bean can wait in the car for a few minutes."

"No, we'll all go in," Mom said firmly. "Whether or not we foster these puppies has to be a family decision. I wish your dad could be here, too, but he's on duty at the firehouse. He said I can vote for him." She pulled up in front of a little white house. "Anyway, here we are."

Lizzie unclipped her seat belt and got up to open the van's sliding door.

"Hold on," said her mom. "Just remember, we're not taking these puppies home today—and we're not taking them at all unless we all agree. Plus, we need to make sure the puppies can deal with a big family like ours. Understood?"

"Understood," chorused Lizzie, Charles, and the Bean.

Lizzie smiled at the Bean as she unbuckled her brother's car seat. He was so great with all their foster puppies! Even though he was only a toddler, he understood how to be quiet and calm and gentle, especially when he was first meeting a puppy. And Charles—well, they didn't call him the Puppy Whisperer for nothing. He really had a way with puppies.

"Come on, guys," she said. Her brothers weren't so bad. "Let's go meet these pups." They all piled out of the car.

The front door flew open before Lizzie and her family even got to the porch. "Oh, man, am I glad to see you," said the woman standing there. There was a toddler clinging to her knee and a baby in her arms, and she looked—well, she looked exhausted. And frazzled. Her hair stuck out in weird clumps, and there was baby food—or maybe baby throw-up—on her shirt. She was wearing two different shoes on her feet: one sneaker and one slipper. Still, she was smiling.

She shook her head as she waved them inside. "I knew Julie would come through for me. She knows the best people." Her baby wailed, and she bounced him up and down as she strode down the hall. She turned back to look at them and laughed. "I know, I know. It's a mess."

The house looked like a tornado had hit it. Lizzie saw a baby sock draped on the bannister. There was a half-eaten bowl of cereal on the floor. Chewed-up dog toys lay all around, and an overflowing basket of laundry sat in the hallway.

"I just can't keep up," said Tracy. "Between the puppies and the kids—and now I have another litter of puppies coming any minute." She threw up her hands. "My cousin said it would be easy. It would be fun. I'd make tons of money." She rolled her eyes. "Meanwhile, I get people who say they want a puppy and never show up, or change their minds. And I've got these two puppies that should have been in their forever homes weeks ago. But nobody wants two at once, and these two are like glue with each other. How can I let them go to separate households?"

She had stopped in front of a baby gate that closed off the kitchen from the rest of the house.

Lizzie and her brothers walked up to peek inside. "Oh!" said Lizzie, putting a hand over her mouth. If anything, the kitchen was even more of a wreck than the rest of the house. Pots and pans were piled on the counters, the sink was overflowing with dishes, and there seemed to be a dusting of flour all over everything. Plus, the floor was covered with newspapers, and the newspapers were covered with—*well*, thought Lizzie, *puppies do have to poop. And pee.*

But Lizzie barely noticed any of that. She was too busy gazing at the two adorable puppies curled up on a bed next to their beautiful mama. The mother looked up at Lizzie and her brothers, but the puppies were still snoozing. Quickly, Lizzie spun around and put her finger on her lips, telling her brothers to be quiet. Then she turned back to gaze at the pups.

"Wow," she said. "Mom, look at them. They're

so, so cute." The puppies had silky white coats with brown splotches, and floppy ears. They slept with their feathery tails curled around their round, pink puppy bellies; Lizzie could tell that these pups had just had a big meal. "And whoa, check it out!" she added. "Their coloring is almost the same." She pointed. Each puppy had a brown splotch outlining her right eye; another, bigger round brown marking on her back and belly; and just a tiny dab of brown at the very end of her tail.

"Actually," Tracy said, "as far as I can tell their coloring is exactly the same." She grinned and held up her hands. "Twins! The vet said dogs don't really have twins the way people do, but you know what? I can't really tell these two apart. Not by looking, anyway."

"What do you mean?" Lizzie asked. "How else would you tell them apart?"

"Oh, by their personalities," said Tracy. "Zig is much braver than her sister. She's the one who would be charging toward us if she was awake. Zag would wait to see how that turned out, and then maybe decide it was safe to come over."

"Zig and Zag! I love those names." Lizzie glanced up at her mom, eyebrows raised. Tracy obviously cared about these dogs, but—also obviously—she really needed help. Lizzie could tell that her mom was thinking the same thing.

"Well, they seem pretty calm, anyway," said Mom.

Lizzie could tell that her mom's heart had melted as soon as she saw the little cuties. Who could resist them?

"Sure, after some exercise and a good meal," said Tracy. "But—"

Lizzie popped her eyes at Tracy, like she was saying "Stop right there!" Mom really needed to believe that these would be mellow pups. Then, out loud, she said, "We can take them and help find them homes. Right, Mom?"

"Well—" said Mom.

"I could sure use the help," Tracy said, sighing as she shifted the baby in her arms. "I'm not cut out for puppy breeding, that is crystal clear."

Lizzie started to say something, something not very nice. She just couldn't understand why anybody would think that breeding puppies was an easy or good way to make money. But she bit her lip and held it in. She really, really wanted to foster these puppies.

"You've just got a lot on your plate," Mom said, giving Tracy a sympathetic look.

Lizzie and Charles shot each other tiny secret grins. They knew their mother couldn't resist helping out another mom who was struggling. That was the moment that Lizzie knew the puppies were coming home with them, after all.

Soon Lizzie was getting back into the van, two soft and very sleepy puppies zipped up inside her jacket. As she settled into her seat, she felt one of them stirring. A moment later, a little white head popped out of the jacket. "Well, hello," said Lizzie. "You must be Zig."

CHAPTER FOUR

"Whoa, look at them go!" Charles said.

The puppies were not sleepy anymore. Zig and Zag—or was it Zag and Zig?—had woken up the second Mom pulled the van into the driveway. They wriggled and squirmed and made happy little puppy noises as they tried to climb out of Lizzie's jacket.

Lizzie and her brothers had taken them right out back into the fenced yard. That was their routine, what they always did with new foster puppies. It was a safe place, and a good way for them to begin to get to know their new, temporary home. It was also a perfect place for new puppies to meet Buddy for the first time. Now, Zig and Zag zoomed around, tumbling and wrestling with each other. Their ears flapped and their tongues hung out as they raced up and down.

Whee! What fun!
Yes! We've been cooped up for too long.

"Those are some happy pups," said Charles. "Just look how fast they are!"

Lizzie grinned. "I know," she said. "I have a feeling they could probably run like this for hours."

Then Mom let Buddy out the back door. "Sit down," Lizzie told her brothers, pulling them over to the wide stairs coming down from the deck. "Let's see how they all do together, without getting in their way."

Buddy came right down the stairs. He was

never afraid of other dogs, unless they growled or snapped at him. One of the puppies charged straight toward Buddy, feathery tail held high and ears flapping.

"That must be Zig, the brave one," said Lizzie. "Look at the other pup. Zag. She's acting exactly the way Tracy described she would." The other puppy stood perfectly still in the middle of the yard, ears on alert as she watched her sister.

Zig screeched to a halt right in front of Buddy and dove into a play bow—butt in the air and front legs on the ground.

Hey, hey, hey! Who are you? Wanna play?

Zag waited and watched—then, as soon as she saw Buddy go into a play bow of his own, she trotted over to join the party.

Well, I guess it's safe—maybe we'll even have some fun!

Soon all three puppies were dashing around the yard, stopping to wrestle and roll around on the newly raked grass. Lizzie laughed. "They're having a great time," she said. "Good thing, too. It'll tire them out."

It should have—but it didn't.

The puppies were still full of high spirits when Lizzie and her brothers brought them inside to see the house and settle down. It was almost suppertime—for people and for dogs. Lizzie scooped up the puppy who'd been leading the chase around the yard. "You must be Zig," she said.

"No, that's Zag," said Charles, who had picked up the other puppy. "This is Zig. Remember? She's the one who grabbed those flowers and made the others chase her."

"Shhh." Lizzie put her finger over her lips. Dad had just bought those two potted chrysanthemums last weekend. Once the puppies had finished tearing the pretty copper-colored flowers to pieces, Lizzie had picked up the stems and petals and buried them into the compost heap. "Dad doesn't need to hear about that, does he? I'm sure they won't do it again." She adjusted the puppy in her arms. "Okay, maybe you're Zag," she said. "Either way, let's all go inside and have a little nap before supper."

Buddy headed straight for his bed in the living room, curled up into a tiny ball, and fell asleep. But Zig and Zag did not seem to know what "nap" meant. Zig squirmed out of Charles's arms, ran to Buddy's toy basket, and pulled out Mr. Duck, Buddy's oldest, most favorite toy. She shook it fiercely and then took off around the living room, hopping up onto the couch and back down again.

Then she turned and cocked her head at her sister, who was taking a moment to get used to the new place after Lizzie had set her down.

Zig let out a few short yips.

Check it out, check it out! Come help me tear this thing apart!

Lizzie looked toward the kitchen, hoping Mom hadn't heard the barking. Oops. There she stood, an oven mitt over one hand, frowning at the noise.

"It's okay," Lizzie said. "I'm sure they won't bark much once—" She was interrupted by a cascade of yips from the puppy at her feet, the one they thought was Zag. Zag took off toward her sister, following the same path up and over the couch, then grabbed one of Mr. Duck's wings with her tiny, sharp teeth. She dug in all four paws and pulled as hard as she could.

I may be shy, but I'm strong!

Lizzie heard a tearing sound just as Zag sat down with a bump, looking surprised at the fuzzy wing—now unattached from Mr. Duck—in her mouth.

"Hoo, boy," said Charles. "Buddy isn't going to be happy about that when he wakes up."

"And I'm not happy about it, either," said Mom. She had come over to see what all the fuss was, and now she shook her head at the adorable pair. Zig and Zag looked at her with big, innocent eyes. But Mom's heart was not so easily melted this time. She gave Lizzie a stern look. "You and your brothers are really going to have to step up and keep these puppies busy—or we won't be able to keep them, even for another day," she said. Then she strode back into the kitchen, still shaking her head.

CHAPTER FIVE

"Wait! Zig—I mean Zag, no! Oh, now you're all tangled up with each other and with Tank. Can't you two stop moving for one second?" Lizzie wanted to cry. She felt a nudge against her hip, and a warm nose snuffled at her hand. She looked down and smiled as she scratched the big German shepherd between the ears. "Oh, Tank, you're the best. If only I could be as patient as you are!"

Lizzie and her friends had a dog-walking business, and Tank was one of the dogs on Lizzie's route. She knew that some people might think this dog was scary, with his long nose, alert ears, and tall, strong body. But Lizzie knew he was the sweetest dude around, a true gentle giant. Tank was always fantastic with the foster puppies Lizzie introduced him to.

Now, he stood as still as a statue while Zig and Zag ran circles around him, tangling their leashes into impossible knots. They nipped at his ankles and pawed at his tail, but he didn't even blink.

"Ugh, maybe Maria was right; this wasn't such a good idea," Lizzie said out loud.

Lizzie had talked to her best friend the night before, telling Maria that she planned to take the new puppies along when she did her dog-walking route the next day. "By then, Mom will definitely need to have them out of the house for a few hours," Lizzie had said. "So will Buddy. They're wearing him out. Sometimes he looks at me like 'Please, help me!'"

"But—will it be okay with all your clients?" Maria had asked.

"I've e-mailed everybody and explained that I've got new foster puppies who need to be socialized, and all but one said yes," said Lizzie. Socializing was when puppies met other dogs and people. Lizzie knew that it was so important for puppies this age.

"Let me guess: Cinnamon's mom," Maria had said. "She's the one who said no."

Lizzie laughed. Little Cinnamon, a teacup Yorkie, was so spoiled and worried over by the woman who owned her. Lizzie practically had to carry Cinnamon down the street to do her business; she wasn't allowed to sniff anything, chase anything, meet any other dogs, eat any snacks that Lizzie brought, or even take a new route around the block.

"You nailed it," she told her friend. "Even

though I promised her that Zig and Zag are super friendly, super healthy, and have all their shots. I'll walk her after I meet up with you at the end of our routes. Maybe you can hold Zig and Zag for a few minutes while I get Cinnamon out."

"I can't wait!" Maria said. "I've never met twin puppies before."

"I'm not sure I ever want to again," Lizzie had said on the phone. At that moment, after a long evening of puppy-wrangling, she was exhausted. "Just kidding . . . sort of. They are a real handful. But"—she glanced down at Zig and Zag, curled up together on her bed—"they sure are cute. When they're sleeping."

Now, out on their walk the next day, Lizzie reached down to pick up each puppy in turn, unclipping each of their leashes as she did her best to undo the tangle they'd made. Tank waited patiently as Lizzie fixed his leash, too. How had two small puppies made such a big tangle? "Zig, I bet you're the ringleader of this whole thing," she said as she clipped the leash back onto a blue collar. Zig looked up at her, frowning a little as if concentrating.

Maybe. Honestly, I can't remember, with all the excitement.

"And Zag, you'll do anything your sister dares you to do, won't you?" She straightened Zag's red collar as the little puppy tried to lick her face.

That's right! 'Cause we're sisters and best friends, too!

The collars had been Charles's brilliant idea, after dinner the night before. "Why don't we put different-colored collars on them, so we can tell them apart?" He'd rummaged through their supply of puppy stuff: a big carton full of leashes, collars, toys, blankets, and food dishes that had been donated by friends. "Here!" he'd said. "Zig, you're blue. And Zag, you can be red!"

Lizzie still wasn't sure if Charles had picked the right puppy for each collar—for that matter, she still couldn't always remember whether Zig was blue or red—but still, it was a good idea. She was sure she'd have an easier time telling the puppies apart once she'd gotten to know them better.

"Plus, there must be something different in your coloring," she said to the pups now as they dropped off Tank and headed down the street to her next client's house. "I haven't found it yet, but I will." Comparing the two puppies was like trying to figure out one of those puzzles where there are supposedly five differences between two pictures, but at first you can't find any.

By the time she met Maria at the end of her route, Lizzie was dragging. Having two rambunctious puppies along had made her route seem twice as long as usual, and she hadn't even walked Cinnamon yet!

"You can say it," she said to Maria as they met on the corner of Maple and Vine.

"Say what?" Maria asked. She had knelt down to scoop the puppies into her arms, and now they were each licking one of her cheeks. She giggled.

"Say 'I told you so,'" said Lizzie. "You were a hundred percent right. There's no way I can take these puppies along on my route every day."

"Which one is this?" Maria asked, petting one tiny brown-and-white head.

"Zig," Lizzie said. "No, Zag. Oh, I don't know." She threw up her hands.

"They sure are cute," said Maria as the puppies climbed all over her. "But if they really can't be separated, it's not going to be easy to find them a home. You may have them for a while."

Lizzie groaned. "I think I'll have to ask Brianna to cover my route," she said. Brianna and Daphne were the other two people in Lizzie and Maria's dog-walking business. Lizzie knew that Brianna had just lost a client when they moved away. "I promised my mom I'd tire Zig and Zag out at least twice a day. I got up an hour early today to play with them in the yard, but they're going to need plenty of exercise in the afternoons, too." She knelt down to give the puppies a pat. "But where—and how?"

Maria looked thoughtful. "I have an idea," she said.

CHAPTER SIX

The next afternoon, Lizzie stood by a fence post, a huge smile on her face. Inside a large fenced area, dozens of dogs ran free with one another. They raced, they wrestled, they sniffed, and they wagged. Some seemed overwhelmed and stuck close to their owners. Others, running wild in the midst of a pack, looked as if they might have forgotten they ever *had* owners. Lizzie loved to see dogs run and play like this. *This was the way dogs were meant to be*, she thought as she watched the scene.

This was Maria's idea: the new dog park, over by the bike path. Lizzie hardly ever walked in that direction, and she'd almost forgotten about

it. Obviously it would be a great place for puppies to socialize while getting exercise. She still
couldn't believe she hadn't thought of it. If Zig
and Zag were tiring out Buddy—and they definitely were—having a whole park full of dogs to
play with was just the thing.

Lizzie hoped it was, anyway. She needed to fix
this before Mom lost her mind. These puppies were
really a handful. When Lizzie had arrived home
from school that day, Mom had met her at the front
door. She'd handed Lizzie her dog-walking backpack and two leashes: Zig's and Zag's. "There's
an apple and a couple of granola bars in the backpack," Mom said as the puppies greeted Lizzie with
yips and yaps and lots of jumping. "That should be
enough to hold you till dinner."

Now, at the dog park, Lizzie felt something
scrabbling at her right leg and looked down to see
Zig, in her blue collar.

What's the big holdup? Don't we get to play?

Lizzie laughed. "You can't wait to be in there, can you?" she asked. "But let's give your sister a chance to get used to the whole scene, so she's not too overwhelmed when we go inside the fence." Lizzie knew that this was what her Aunt Amanda did when she introduced a new dog at her doggy day care. "Some dogs just aren't ready to plunge right in," Aunt Amanda always said.

Lizzie felt a scrabbling at her left leg. Zag looked up at her, eyes sparkling.

I think I'm almost ready to join the fun!

"Oh, now you want to play, too?" Lizzie laughed.
"Cute puppies," said someone behind her.
Lizzie felt herself blushing as she turned to see

who had spoken. She was embarrassed to be caught talking out loud to her dogs. A young woman with bangs and chin-length black hair sat on a nearby bench, a large sketchpad across her lap.

"And you're great with them," the woman added.

Lizzie felt better. Some people understood about talking to dogs. She craned her neck a bit, trying to get a look at what the woman was drawing, but Zig and Zag both chose that moment to pull at their leashes, tugging her toward the gate into the dog park.

Let's go! What are we waiting for?

"Whoops!" said Lizzie. "Guess it's time to go play." She grinned over her shoulder at the black-haired woman as the puppies dragged her along.

The dog park had a special type of double gate

to make sure no dogs escaped. Once you'd opened the first gate, you were in a sort of holding pen. After you'd closed the outside gate, you could open the inside one and let your dogs loose. "Ready, you two?" Lizzie asked as she unclipped their leashes. "I'll be right here if you need me."

She opened the second gate and Zig and Zag zoomed off, sticking together like glue. First they ran up to a dog their size, some sort of terrier, Lizzie thought. All three dogs took a moment to sniff one another, and then they bounced off together, racing up and down in the fenced yard. All along the way Zig and Zag kept stopping to meet other dogs, until a gang of five or six was charging around like a herd of tiny buffalo.

Lizzie knew that dog parks weren't always perfect places for every dog. Some dogs didn't know how to play nicely, and they could ruin it for other, shyer dogs. But so far, this park seemed like a happy place. People stood around chatting while they watched their dogs play, or threw balls for their dogs to catch, or just sat off to the side with quieter dogs, watching the action.

Lizzie shook her head. How could she have forgotten how much fun the dog park could be? It was like heaven for a dog-crazy person. She spotted a wolfhound, a chow, five Labs (three black, one yellow, and one chocolate), and two beagles. She saw a galumphing St. Bernard playing with a tiny Pomeranian.

And then, over in the far corner, she saw a handful of people standing and talking as they watched a bunch of puppies romp and wrestle. Her people! Puppy people! Keeping an eye on Zig and Zag, Lizzie headed for that corner. Zig would probably have played all day without even noticing where she had gone, but luckily Zag was watching Lizzie more carefully.

Come on! She's going this way. Let's stick with her. It's safer.

Both dogs dashed after Lizzie, then passed her when they spotted the other puppies. They jumped right into the mix, rolling and tumbling and chasing and play-biting.

Whee! This is the best!

"Hi," said a woman in a bright red jacket. "Welcome! Did you sign up online?"

"Sign up?" Lizzie asked. "For what?"

"Puppy kindergarten," said the woman. "It's just an informal class, but we do ask people to check in." She reached out her hand for a shake. "I'm Eleanor," she said. "I'm the teacher, sort of. But really, we're all learning together."

"I'm Lizzie," said Lizzie. "And I'm so sorry to

disrupt your class. I didn't even know about it. I'm fostering these puppies, and I just brought them here so they could play. They have so much energy and they're driving my mom—and my own puppy—kind of nuts."

Eleanor waved a hand. "No problem! Like I said, it's very informal. You're welcome to join us anytime—including today. And disruptions are part of the idea. The puppies need to learn to deal with distractions." She raised her voice and spoke to the group. "This would be a good time to call your puppies over and ask them to sit," she said. "And remember, if they don't come the first time you call, just go get them. Don't keep calling over and over—if you do, they'll just learn to tune you out."

Lizzie watched as the people separated from one another and called their puppies. Obviously, these pups had already learned a lot. Four of them trotted right over to their people. Two others couldn't quite tear themselves away from playing with the new girls, Zig and Zag.

"Come, Zig!" Lizzie called. "Come, Zag!" She bent down and opened her arms wide.

Zag came running, but Zig lingered, still playing with a floppy-eared fluffy poodle pup. Lizzie went to get her. "You've got a lot to learn," she murmured into the puppy's ear, when she'd scooped her up. "And I think we just found the perfect place for that!"

CHAPTER SEVEN

"You know the best part about this?" Lizzie asked Maria as they headed for the dog park together the next afternoon, right after school.

"The dogs?" Maria asked.

"Well, yes," said Lizzie, giggling. "The dogs, of course. And being with you. I'm so glad you decided to ask Brianna and Daphne to cover your dog-walking route, too, so you could help me with these two." She gestured down at the puppies. The one with the blue collar, who Lizzie had finally learned to remember was Zig, was at the end of the leash Lizzie held, and Zag, in her red collar, was at the end of Maria's. "Eleanor, the trainer, did seem to suggest pretty strongly that it would be better this way, with each of the pups having her own handler."

Zig pranced ahead of them with her tail held high, noticing everything as she trotted by. She tossed her head as she looked back at Lizzie.

I think I know where we're going—and I can't wait!

Meanwhile, Zag walked closer to Maria's side, glancing up at her from time to time.

I'm glad you're along, too. It makes me feel safer to have two nice people with me.

"Okay, but what's the *other* best part?" Maria asked, teasingly.

"Oh, that," said Lizzie. "Getting out of raking, of course! Now Charles has to finish cleaning up the yard, since it's much more important for me to get the puppies out for more exercise and training." She held up her hand, and Maria smacked it.

The scene at the dog park was just as busy as it had been the day before. Lizzie and Maria stood by the fence for a moment before they went in to join the puppy kindergarten group.

"Hey, cuties!" The black-haired woman Lizzie had seen yesterday walked up, set her backpack on the nearby bench, and then came over to pet the puppies. "I was hoping I'd see these two adorable puppies again today."

"Do you come here every day?" Lizzie asked.

The woman, who was now kneeling on the ground with two happy puppies climbing over her, nodded. "Pretty much. I walk here on the bike path, from Northfield."

Lizzie was impressed. That was the next town over, a couple of miles away at least. "But you don't even have a dog," she blurted out, realizing too late that she sounded a bit rude. Maria poked her in the ribs and rolled her eyes.

The woman laughed. "I used to, but it's been a while. My dachshund, Freddy, died a year ago. I do think about getting another—the time just hasn't been right yet. But I love watching and drawing the dogs."

"Lizzie!" Lizzie looked up to see Eleanor, the puppy kindergarten teacher, waving at her. "Come join us!"

"Coming!" Lizzie waved back. "Better go," she called out as she let Zig pull her toward the gate. "But maybe tomorrow we can see some of your drawings."

The woman gave her a thumbs-up. "I'm Anne," she said. "I'd be happy to show you—and I'd love to draw your puppies one day."

"They're not really mine. I'm just fostering them," Lizzie said while dashing after Zig.

"I'm glad you brought a friend today," Eleanor said, when Maria and Lizzie joined her group. "That'll make everything a lot easier. Today we're going to be working on the 'leave it' command, and that can be challenging."

"You mean, like, if they see something on the ground that they want to gobble up?" Lizzie asked. She had worked on the "leave it" command with Buddy.

Elcanor nodded. "Or a squirrel they want to chase," she added. "For this excrcise we'll keep our puppies on their leashes. But I'm thinking that maybe these pups could use some playtime, first."

"Zig and Zag could play all day, every day," Lizzie agreed.

"We'll let everyone run for a while before the lesson, then," Eleanor said, raising her voice so the others could hear. "Release your puppies!"

Maria and Lizzie unclipped the puppies' leashes and watched, laughing, as Zig and Zag threw themselves into puppy playtime. Zig ran straight for the biggest puppy, a solidly built bulldog, and jumped onto her back. The bulldog took off at a run like a bucking bronco with a cowgirl aboard, and Zig grinned back at her sister.

Come on! It's fun and there's room for both of us!

"Oh, my," Eleanor said to Lizzie as she watched Zag dash over to join the game. "You've got a lot on your hands, don't you? I'm glad you've joined our group."

"So am I," said Lizzie. "And honestly? So is my

mom. She really appreciated the way they conked out yesterday after playing here." Then she took a deep breath. Why not just go ahead and ask?

"Remember how I told you that my family is fostering these puppies? Maybe you'd be interested in adopting them." Lizzie saw Eleanor start to shake her head, but she kept going. "I really don't think they should be separated. So they have to stay together, and not everybody could handle that, but you seem to know a lot about dogs, and training, and all that stuff. I'm sure you could deal with a pair of high-energy puppies. I mean—" Lizzie knew she was talking too fast and too much, but she couldn't stop. This might be her best chance to convince Eleanor to adopt Zig and Zag. She had to grab the moment.

Eleanor held up a hand, laughing. "Thanks, but I think my partner would kill me, especially since we just adopted a puppy of our own." She waved toward a corner of the dog park. "That's Flora, my bulldog, over there with your two—"

She stopped in mid-sentence and put her hand over her mouth. "Oh, no," she groaned. "Looks like they found the mud pit."

CHAPTER EIGHT

"Keep that door closed," Lizzie warned Charles. "We have to try to get these puppies cleaned up before Mom sees them." Lizzie and her brother were in the downstairs bathroom later that afternoon, with two very muddy puppies. Lizzie and Maria had finished the lesson at the dog park that afternoon—after all, they still had to tire the puppies out—but now it was time to wash off all the crusted mud that Zig and Zag had rolled in.

Lizzie was struggling with a wriggly Zig as she tried to fill the big sink with warm water. They were using this bathroom instead of the upstairs one, which had a bathtub—which would have made a lot more sense and would have made things a lot easier—because Mom's office was right down the hall from that bathroom, and she was in the middle of a long interview over the phone. This way, they wouldn't interrupt her. And maybe, if they were lucky, Mom would never know what a mess the puppies had gotten into.

"But why does the dog park even have a mud pit, anyway?" Charles asked, as he tried to hold Zag tightly without getting covered with dried mud himself.

"It doesn't usually," Lizzie said. "Eleanor told us that it appeared after those big rainstorms last week. Of course, all the dogs love it. Eleanor said that today will be the third day in a row she'll have to give her bulldog Flora a bath." She checked the temperature of the water. "Okay, missy," she said. "We're going in." She lifted Zig over the sink. The puppy splayed out her feet, trying to avoid the water. "It's okay, it's nice and warm," Lizzie said soothingly. "Here we go." She looked at Charles. "We can take their collars off as long as we don't let go of the puppies. I know this is Zig, and you have Zag. Those collars need a good scrubbing, too."

She dipped the puppy into the water and held her carefully as she scrubbed her all over. Mud-colored suds soon filled the sink.

"You might as well get Zag in here, too," said Lizzie. "We'll have to run another sinkful to rinse them."

Water sloshed onto the floor as the puppies squirmed and wriggled. The water turned dark brown. Suds flew into Lizzie's face and dripped down her front. Charles had a big smear of mud on his cheek. "This is good," Lizzie said, panting a little as she reached out one hand to drag a couple of towels off the rack and throw them onto the floor. "Almost done." She scrubbed at one last spot on Zig's pink tummy until she realized that it wasn't mud at all, just a freckle. Then she pushed down the knob to let the water drain out.

The two puppies stood in the sink as muddy water receded around them. They both looked like skinny, wet rats. Clumps of fur and mud were spattered everywhere. Zig looked up at Lizzie, shivering a little.

Um, was that really necessary? Are we done now?

Then, without warning, she scrambled out of the sink, hopped down onto the closed toilet, and ran to scratch at the door. A second later, Zag squirmed out of Charles's grasp and followed her. She joined her sister at the door, whining and yipping.

We gotta get out of this place!!

"Well, at least they can't get out," said Lizzie—just as the bathroom door opened.

"What is going on in here?" Mom asked, staring at the mess. The Bean stood behind her, his mouth wide open in surprise. Next to him was Buddy, looking curious about the fuss. The puppies dodged past them all, dripping muddy suds as they raced out of reach.

Lizzie felt like crying. She had just been trying to do the right thing, and now there were two dirty, soapy, wet puppies running around the house. "The puppies—mud pit—get them!" was all she could manage to say. She couldn't seem to make whole sentences come out of her mouth. Lizzie pushed past her mother and ran after the puppies. "Zig!" she called. "Zag!"

Lizzie was exhausted by the time the Petersons sat down to dinner. It had taken hours to catch the puppies, rinse them, dry them, and then clean up the disaster zone of the bathroom. Once they were done with all that, Mom had sent Lizzie and Charles upstairs to change their clothes before she would let them sit down to eat their grilled cheese sandwiches and tomato soup. (Which was what Mom usually cooked when she didn't feel like cooking and Dad was on a shift down at the fire station.)

Zig and Zag, or possibly Zag and Zig (of course, their collars had gotten mixed up in all the excitement), had finally realized that they were way overdue for a nap. Once they were clean and dry and had eaten some dinner, they curled up together on the bed next to Buddy's and fell fast asleep. Lizzie heard their tiny snores as she came back downstairs in a clean, dry sweatshirt and leggings.

"Well," Mom said as she ladled out tomato soup,

"what have we learned from this whole episode?"

Lizzie and Charles groaned. Mom was always trying to point out "teachable moments." Couldn't something just happen, without there having to be a whole lesson in it?

Mom ignored the groans, passed out sandwiches, and waited for an answer. She was being very calm and patient. In a way, Lizzie would rather she just yelled at them and got it over with. This was much more work. Lizzie took a bite of her sandwich, thinking. What had she learned? "I guess I should have kept a closer eye on Zig and Zag at the dog park," she said. "So they didn't get into the mud in the first place."

"Mm, hmm," Mom said. She turned to Charles, eyebrows raised. "And you? Any lessons?"

"Um, lock the bathroom door if you're giving two puppies a bath?" he asked, shrugging.

Lizzie burst out laughing, but Mom just nodded.

"Okay," Mom said. "Both good thoughts. But here's what I think is the real lesson." She paused, taking a sip of soup. Then she sat up straight and held up her index finger. "Don't. Foster. Two. Puppies. At. A. Time," she said.

"Oh," said Lizzie. That was not the lesson she'd learned, but okay. She had to admit that Mom might have a little bit of a point. Two puppies really could be a whole lot of work, like much more than twice the amount of work that one puppy took. Still, Lizzie was determined to keep fostering Zig and Zag until she could find them the perfect home.

"And if you really have to foster two pups at once," Mom continued, holding out her arms pleadingly. "At least try to figure out how to tell them apart!"

"Ooh!" said Lizzie, sitting up straight. "I just remembered! I think I know how to do that!"

CHAPTER NINE

"Come on," Lizzie said, jumping up from her seat at the dinner table. "I'll show you."

"Wait," said Mom, following her into the living room. "Are you sure you want to wake Zig and Zag when they're finally sleeping?"

But it was too late. Lizzie had already picked up one of the sleepy puppies. "See?" she said. She cradled the puppy gently so that her round, pink belly was showing. "Look! This is Zig. She has a freckle under her right front leg!" The puppy squirmed sleepily and yawned, pawing at her face.

Hello? I'm trying to get some rest here.

Mom picked up Zag and examined her belly. "And this puppy doesn't. So she must be Zag." Zag yawned, too, letting out a little squeal.

Can't a puppy get some peace and quiet?

"Quick, can you get the collars?" Lizzie said to Charles. "They're in the bathroom. I washed them and hung them on the towel rack to dry."

Charles ran to the bathroom and came back with the two collars. Lizzie put the blue one on Zig, and Mom put the red one on Zag. "Now we'll always know," said Lizzie.

"Blue, Zig. Red, Zag," the Bean chanted. He really was getting good at his colors.

"Well, that's better," said Mom. "But even though we can tell them apart now, I'm not sure how much longer we can care for them. You have no idea how disruptive they are when

I'm trying to work while you're at school."

Lizzie nuzzled the puppy in her arms. Zig had gone back to sleep and she was so soft and warm. "I know, I know," she said. "But I think the puppy group is really helping. See how they're sleeping now? It really tires them out, plus, they're learning so much. Please, just a couple more days? I'm sure the right owner will come along." Lizzie held up Zig and made her paw wave a little. "Please?" she repeated, in a pretend puppy voice, high and squeaky. "Can't we stay a little longer?"

Mom smiled, then lowered her face and rubbed her cheek on Zag's soft fur. "Well . . ." she said.

"Phew," said Maria, the next day. She and Lizzie were walking to Lizzie's house after school, to pick up the puppies and head to the dog park. "So, you get to keep them a little longer?"

"Yes!" said Lizzie. She shivered and pulled up her hood. It was a gray day, and just as they'd left school it had started to drizzle, or mist, or whatever. Mizzle. It was not a nice day at all, and Lizzie would have loved to go home and curl up on the couch with the puppies. She was in the middle of a really good book, called *From the Mixed-Up Files of Mrs. Basil E. Frankweiler*, about some kids who ran away and lived in a museum. How nice it would be to read a few chapters under a cozy blanket. Much nicer than going back out in the rain and coming home again with a pair of muddy puppies.

But no. That wasn't going to happen. When she got home, she knew that instead of sleepy, cozy puppies, she would find a couple of wired, hyper, ready-to-go pups—plus one frazzled mom— waiting for her. It was her job to take those pups and tire them out, mud or no mud. "Thanks so, so much for coming with me again today," Lizzie started to say to Maria, just as a car horn honked behind them.

It was Maria's dad. "Maria, did you forget?" he asked. He pulled over and leaned out of the car window. "You have a dentist appointment. We're going to be late!"

Maria gave Lizzie a horrified look. "Oh, no, I'm so sorry," she said. She ran to throw her backpack into the car and jump in after it. "But you can do it!" she called back to Lizzie. "You can handle those pups on your own."

Lizzie felt her shoulders sag. Sure, she could do it. But at that very moment, if she was honest? She didn't want to. It was hard enough to have to be out on a cold, wet day. But handling both Zig and Zag? That made it even harder. "Bye," Lizzie called as Maria and her dad drove out of sight. She trudged home. Maybe Charles could help.

"Nope," her mom said, shaking her head, when Lizzie got home and asked. "Charles worked really hard at raking yesterday so I said he could go to the arcade today with Sammy and his dad."

Lizzie sighed. Zig and Zag were already scrabbling at the door, dying to get out. They loved playing with the other puppies and didn't care one bit about the weather, or mud, or anything else. Zig ran back and forth from the door to Lizzie.

Are we going? When? Now? Let's go now!

Zag, meanwhile, just sat at the door and whined.

I'm bored! We've been hanging around all day. It's time for some fun.

Lizzie couldn't help herself. She burst out laughing, her bad mood forgotten. Sure, these puppies were a lot of work, but they were so adorable, so happy, so energetic, so ready for anything. "You guys!" she said, giggling. "Okay, let's go." She snapped on their leashes and grabbed her dog-walking backpack.

Mom looked relieved as she walked them out onto the porch. "Maybe you should wear your rain jacket," she said, gazing up at the heavy gray clouds.

"I'll be fine," said Lizzie. Now that she was ready to go, she was ready to go.

Mom lifted her hands. "If it starts pouring, I'll come pick you up," she said.

"Bye!" Lizzie said, feeling a whole lot happier as she headed off. Puppies had a way of making bad moods disappear.

When she arrived at the dog park, Lizzie saw Anne wiping off her usual bench with a hand-ful of paper towels. She wore a bright yellow rain jacket, and her black hair was tucked beneath a green baseball hat. "Hi! Where's your friend today?" she asked, when she saw Lizzie. She knelt to pet Zig and Zag.

"Dentist," Lizzie said, making a face.

"Ick," said Anne. "So, maybe you need some help with these two today?"

Lizzie nodded eagerly. "Can you? Would you?"

"Sure," said Anne. "I'm sure I can handle Zag, anyway, if you take Zig." She held up the puppy in the red collar.

"You can tell them apart?" Lizzie asked, surprised.

"Of course!" said Anne. "Zig is the wild one. Zag is much shyer."

"Wow, you've really been paying attention," said Lizzie.

Anne shrugged. "That's what artists do," she said. "We notice things."

"Cool," said Lizzie. "And guess what?" she asked as they headed for the gate. "Remember how muddy they got yesterday? Well, when we were washing them I found a freckle on Zig's belly—so now we can always tell them apart."

"Fantastic," said Anne. She looked up at the sky. "Uh-oh, I think it's starting to—"

And the rain began to pour down.

CHAPTER TEN

"Whoa," said Anne, pulling up the hood on her rain jacket.

Lizzie's sweatshirt was soaked through in seconds. She looked down at the puppy at the end of her leash. Zig looked back at her, big-eyed and shivering.

Do we have to get wet every single day with you?

She and her sister, Zag, looked just like they had after their baths the day before, skinny and dripping. Zag shook herself off and then looked up hopefully at Anne.

Any room under your coat? I'm freezing.

Anne bent down, scooped up the puppy, and tucked her inside her jacket. Lizzie did the same with Zig, even though her sweatshirt wasn't going to offer much protection. "Now what?" she asked.

"Yoo-hoo!" called Eleanor, from the other corner of the park. She waved at them. "We're all heading home. Doesn't look like this rain is going to let up anytime soon."

Then Lizzie heard a car beeping. Mom! "My mother's here," said Lizzie. "Come on. I'm sure she'd want you to come home with us. You can't walk to Northfield in this."

Sure enough, Mom waved them both into the van. "I've got the heat turned all the way up," she said. "Are the puppies okay? Are you?"

"Mom, this is Anne," said Lizzie. "Remember, I

told you about the person who walks all the way from Northfield to draw the dogs?"

"Betsy Peterson," said Mom, introducing herself. "We'll get you back home later, but for now come on and dry off at our place. Lizzie's dad made chili today, so there's plenty for dinner."

"Um—okay, thanks!" said Anne, settling herself in for the way back.

At home, Mom gave Anne some dry clothes to change into. Lizzie and Charles rubbed the puppies with old towels until they were dry and fluffy. They still smelled good from their bath the day before. And best of all, even though they hadn't run around much, they seemed tired out from the day's excitement. They curled up on their bed for a nap.

Anne sat down on the floor near them and pulled her drawing pad out of her backpack. She began to draw Zig and Zag, capturing them in a few quick strokes of her pencil.

Lizzie, Charles, and the Bean gathered around to watch. "You're so good!" said Lizzie as she watched the puppies come to life on the paper.

"It's just a sketch," Anne said. "I've been dying to draw these two."

"Draw me!" said the Bean, patting Anne on the shoulder. "Draw me!"

Anne laughed. "Sure," she said. She turned to face the Bean and flipped to a fresh sheet of drawing paper. "Okay, don't move for a sec." Her pencil moved across the paper as she glanced at him and then back down at her pad. The Bean sat as still as Lizzie had ever seen him, hardly breathing, until Anne turned the pad around to show him.

"Wow!" he said, reaching for it. He marveled over the picture, touching it with his finger. Then he gave the pad back to Anne. "Again!" This time he stood in a superhero pose, arms akimbo and chin held high.

"No, me," said Charles, jumping in front of the Bean in a ninja pose.

"How about me and Buddy?" Lizzie asked. Buddy had emerged from the den, where he had taken to hanging out while the puppies were around. Lizzie pulled him onto her lap and straightened his collar, so that he would look his very best.

Anne drew them all, until Dad called to say that dinner was ready.

"Anne's really good," Charles said. "Show them, Anne."

Anne waved a hand. "It's just something I do for fun," she said. "There's a million artists out there who are better than me."

"I don't know," Mom said, looking over the drawings. "You really have a way of capturing people—and dogs. I should put you in touch with my friend who's the art director at our newspaper. He's always looking for talented artists."

Anne ducked her head. "Thanks," she said. "And thanks for dinner. You folks have been really kind."

After they'd eaten, Mom shooed Anne into the living room. "You relax," she said. "Charles and Lizzie will help clean up, then we'll give you a ride home."

Lizzie raced through clearing the table, then joined Anne. The puppies had woken up and were wrestling and tumbling on the living room floor. Anne's pencil flew as she made sketch after sketch. It wasn't just that she was a good artist, Lizzie thought. It was like she had said: she really *saw* things. Anyone could look at those pictures and know right away which one was Zig and which was Zag. How did she do it? Lizzie studied Anne's face as the young woman watched the puppies. She saw focus and determination— and something else. Lizzie saw love.

"You love them!" she burst out.

Anne grinned. "I think I do," she said. She shrugged, holding up her hands. "Love happens!" She looked back at the puppies. "I was so sure that my next dog was going to be a dachshund like Freddy, my last dog. But now I have a feeling my next dog is going to be—*two* dogs. These two."

Lizzie's heart leapt up. "Really?" she asked. "Are you sure? They're a lot to handle."

Anne laughed. "I know. But I'll manage, some- how. You know I love to take long walks—that'll help tire them out. What do you think?"

"I think it's the best idea ever," said Lizzie. "They'll get to stay together in a wonderful home. Plus, I'll get to see all three of you at the dog park!" She jumped to her feet. She couldn't wait to tell the rest of the family. But first, she scooped up Zig, then Zag, and gave each of them a kiss on the head. "You are two lucky girls," she said.

PUPPY TIPS

As Lizzie found out, two puppies can be more than twice as much work as one! It's a wonderful thing for a dog to grow up with a playmate, but think about it carefully before you adopt siblings. Sometimes brother and sister puppies (or two brothers, or two sisters) can be a special handful. They might be more interested in each other than in the humans in their family, which can make them harder to train. If your family does decide to adopt a pair of siblings, make sure you're ready for some extra work. And extra fun, too, of course!

Dear Reader,

I once fostered two puppies who were brother and sister. They were the cutest puppies, full of spirit and energy. They were also wild and crazy and loved to destroy everything in sight! I had so much fun with them, but I have to say I was a bit relieved when it was time for them to go to their new homes. I think it was better that they were separated, but it was great that they both lived in the same town, so they could get together once in a while.

Yours from the Puppy Place,

Ellen Miles

For another book about sibling puppies, check out SUGAR, GUMMI, AND LOLLIPOP!

ABOUT THE AUTHOR

Ellen Miles loves dogs, which is why she has a great time writing the Puppy Place books. And guess what? She loves cats, too! (In fact, her very first pet was a beautiful tortoiseshell cat named Jenny.) That's why she came up with the Kitty Corner series. Ellen lives in Vermont and loves to be outdoors with her dog, Zipper, every day, walking, biking, skiing, or swimming, depending on the season. She also loves to read, cook, explore her beautiful state, play with dogs, and hang out with friends and family.

Visit Ellen at ellenmiles.net.